MEET THE

Jam Pandas

ILLUSTRATED BY STEPHANIE BOEY

WRITTEN BY CAROLINE REPCHUK

SIENA

It was a sunny afternoon in June when the Jam Pandas arrived at Tumbledown Orchard in a big open truck. As the truck came to a stop outside the front door of the crumbling cottage, the excited pandas jumped out. There were seven of them altogether — Grandma, Ma and Pa Jam, Big Bamboo their eldest son, Peaches and Plum the young twins, and baby Jim Jam.

MA AND PA JAM

PEACHES AND PLUM

BIG BAMBOO

JIM JAM

7

The Jam Pandas had been left the cottage and orchard by their Great Uncle Greengage, who was rather an eccentric old panda. He had spent all of his time tending the fruit in the orchard, and had neglected the cottage, which was badly in need of repair. "Never mind," said Grandma cheerfully. "We'll soon smarten it up." "Come along then, everybody," said Pa. "Let's get this truck unloaded."

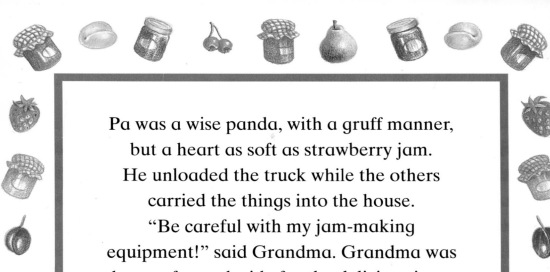

Pa was a wise panda, with a gruff manner,
but a heart as soft as strawberry jam.
He unloaded the truck while the others
carried the things into the house.
"Be careful with my jam-making
equipment!" said Grandma. Grandma was
known far and wide for the delicious jams
she made. "I shall soon be making jam with
all the lovely fruit from the orchard, "
she said happily. "I wonder if there
is a strawberry patch?"
Every Jam Panda had their own
favourite flavour of jam. Grandma's was
strawberry and Pa's was pear.

Soon everything was unloaded, and Ma set about organizing the clean up. Everyone was given a job to do. "This place needs scrubbing from top to bottom!" she said briskly. In no time at all, floors were being scrubbed, carpets were being beaten and feather dusters were flying over the dusty furniture. "I think I'll have earned a nice raspberry jam sandwich after all this hard work," puffed Ma. (*You can guess what flavour jam Ma liked!*)

Ma knew that the cheeky young Jam Panda twins, Peaches and Plum, wanted to explore the rest of the house, so she sent them to look for a good place to store all the jars of jam they had brought with them. The excited little pandas searched through every room in the house, opening cupboards and drawers. The old rooms were dark and dusty and full of cobwebs — just right for hiding in and jumping out on poor Grandma, who was trying to find somewhere to keep her knitting! The terrible twins were always playing tricks and up to mischief.

They chased each other up the stairs.
"Look at me!" cried Peaches, swinging from
the frame of an old four-poster bed.
Soon Peaches and Plum were jumping on
the bed and fighting with the pillows.
Feathers were flying everywhere.
"Jumping Jamspoons!" cried Ma,
coming into the room. "We're supposed
to be cleaning the house, not messing it up!
Go out into the garden and look
after your little brother."

Peaches and Plum went downstairs and into the garden. Their little brother Jim Jam was sitting in the blueberry patch.
There was nothing he liked more than blueberries, especially when they were made into jam! Jim Jam was an adorable little baby panda, who was full of energy. Ma had to keep a close eye on him as he would crawl away whenever he got the chance.

Jim Jam had been eating the berries, and now there was juice running all down his chin. "That looks like fun," said Peaches. Soon the twins were holding a competition to see who could

cram the most blueberries in their mouth at once, and their faces were covered in juice. Just then, Plum looked up. "Uh-oh!" he said, through a mouthful of berries. "Aunt alert!"

Aunt Apricot had arrived with a house-warming gift of an enormous jam sponge. Now she was heading down the garden towards the three young pandas, holding a large handkerchief which she had fished from her handbag. "Jangling jampots! You three are in a jam! Come here and I'll clean you up," she said, licking the corner of her hankie. With that, the three little pandas were off in a flash, heading for the house as fast as their little furry paws could carry them.

Back in the kitchen Big
Bamboo, the eldest son, was
unpacking all the jam they had
brought with them. All of the
jars were open, and he looked
up guiltily as the rest of the
family appeared.

"What are you up to now?"
asked Ma, with a sigh.

"Just testing to make sure
none of the jam went off during
the journey," said Big Bamboo,
innocently. He was such a greedy
panda, especially when it came
to his favourite blackcurrant
jam. "Well I think we've all
earned some tea," said Ma.

And so the Jam Pandas settled down to the first of many jammy teatimes in their new home at Tumbledown Cottage.

"I think we're going to be happy here," said Grandma.

"So do I," said Big Bamboo. "After all, the blackcurrant patch is enormous!"

• T H E   E N D •